MW01145424

The Briny Deep Mysteries

THE BATTLE

The Briny Deep Mysteries Book 3

Jennifer Torres

I'm thankful for so many things.

A late night chat years ago under a sea of stars when my son Timmy and I began to dream up a story about a place called Briny Deep.

My daughter Emily who believed in the story and told me to write it now because the laundry could wait.

*My daughter Isabelle who agreed (begrudgingly) to take a break from her Movie Star Planet computer game so I could actually use **my** computer to write.*

A horrible boss and soul zapping job that made me realize I had to send out what I wrote because my dreams were not going to come find me.

My editors: David Dilkes for believing in me and being the original champion for this story—and the funny, patient, inspiring David Mulrine for all the pep talks and ego boosting emails.

Supportive family members like my dear mother for reading each and every word the minute I wrote it, my Dad, Jim, Danny, Stacey, Matthew, and my sister Natalie.

And finally to my wonderful husband—and fellow dream chaser—John, who refused to hear any more of my "great book ideas" until I actually wrote one to completion. I love you.

Copyright © 2015 by Jennifer Torres.

All rights reserved.

No part of this book may be reproduced by any means without the written permission of the publisher.

Library of Congress Cataloging-in-Publication Data

Torres, Jennifer.
    The battle / Jennifer Torres.
        pages cm. — (The Briny Deep mysteries ; book 3)
    Summary: "With the secret of Briny Deep finally exposed, Tim and his friends must run for their lives. Their journey will take them far away to a strange land where more incredible surprises await. And as a war between two distant lands begins to erupt, Tim must have the courage to dig deeper than he ever has before"—Provided by publisher.
    ISBN 978-1-62285-186-7
    [1. Mystery and detective stories. 2. Friendship—Fiction. 3. Science fiction.] I. Title.
    PZ7.T645648Bat 2014
    [Fic]—dc23   2014000878

Future editions:
Paperback ISBN: 978-1-62285-187-4   EPUB ISBN: 978-1-62285-188-1
Single-User PDF ISBN: 978-1-62285-189-8   Multi-User PDF ISBN: 978-1-62285-190-4

Speeding Star
Box 398, 40 Industrial Road
Berkeley Heights, NJ 07922
USA
www.speedingstar.com

Cover Illustration: © Vadim Sadovski/Shutterstock.com

Contents

Chapter 1

Welcome Home

A catastrophic crash seemed unavoidable.

After such peaceful, quiet space travel, all of a sudden things had begun to change. The gentle hum of the engines that had lulled Tim to sleep when he first boarded the ship was now becoming a deep and increasing rumble.

Light from distant stars streaked across the blackness of space outside the small windows of the spacecraft. It was like they were falling into a dark, bottomless pit.

Tim lifted his head up as everything in the passenger cabin started shaking.

Uh oh, he thought, as he suddenly felt nauseous and dizzy.

He looked over at Max, Emily, and Luke. They each had a look of sheer terror on their face.

"Ugh, I feel like I might throw up," Max said. "Does anyone have a pail?"

Canary ran back to him and handed him a large tube-like thing.

"Throw up in that," he instructed.

Max didn't wait for him to ask twice.

Not a comforting sight.

Tim closed his eyes. After everything he and his friends had been through, entering Earth's atmosphere should be a piece of cake.

Ugh, cake.

The mere thought of it at this moment made him want to retch. His stomach was doing somersaults, and his head was spinning.

Just moments ago, Tim awoke from his well-deserved nap to find Rusty and Canary standing over him. He had slept right through their journey.

"Even though Indus and Earth are far away from each other, the trip itself actually isn't long at all," Canary had explained. "If the conditions are right, we can travel very, very fast using the wormholes in space and before you know it—we're there."

"Wormholes?" Emily asked.

"Yes—they are shortcuts in space," Rusty explained. "Some call them an Einstein–Rosen Bridge."

Rusty got up from his chair and took a piece of paper from a notebook. Then he marked two points with a pencil.

"Imagine that this is space with Indus at one end and Earth at the other," he said pointing at two opposite ends of the paper where the points were made. "Now see what happens when I fold this paper in half?"

"The two points are on top of each other," said Max.

"Exactly," Rusty said. "The wormhole takes us though like this—like a bridge."

The Battle

"You mean we are actually here—at Earth—already?" Tim had asked in disbelief.

Canary had laughed out loud.

"Yes. Welcome home."

But what he hadn't explained is how bumpy the ride through the atmosphere would be.

A sudden sharp dip in altitude jolted Tim back into his seat.

The big comfortable chairs where they sat were equipped with several safety straps for takeoff and landing.

Canary had instructed them to buckle up just moments before the ship got all herky-jerky.

An unrestrained bag of trash slid down the aisle between their seats toward the front of the spacecraft, spilling its contents along the way.

Rusty jumped out of his seat, gathered the garbage in a white bag, and secured it in a cabinet. Then he quickly returned to his seat.

"It's going to get pretty bumpy," Canary called out. "Doing okay back there, Max?"

"Uh . . . define okay," Max called out.

Throughout the whole trip, Max and Canary had definitely bonded. They joked around a lot together. They seemed almost like old friends. It was nice to see this other side of Canary. He was actually a pretty cool guy. What a surprise that was!

Tim turned to look out the window and was able to see the earth—there was a large mass of land covering much of the sea. The bright blue water that seemed so abundant from space now appeared like a mere puddle next to all the solid ground he saw below. But more terrifying than that was the orange-red glow he noticed coming from the outside of the craft—were they on fire?

"Rusty?" Tim called out. "I think there are flames outside the window."

"What did you say?" yelled Max above the roar of the engines.

"It's normal, Max," Canary called out. "We're going to be just fine."

Tim's whole body was so stiff from sitting in the chair. He could barely lift his hand in order to shield his eyes from the terrifying descent.

The ship shook and rumbled. It began to feel as if the whole thing might break apart into a million pieces. He could just picture his chair ripping free, spinning him deep into space where he would float aimlessly away to his ultimate doom.

Tim closed his eyes and tried to get the image out of his head.

Things had changed so much in such a short time. He already missed his parents—or more correctly—he missed the people who had raised him. He would be meeting his real parents soon—on Earth. What would they be like? Did he have brothers and sisters? What if they didn't like him? What if he didn't like them? Thoughts swirled randomly around his brain, a welcome distraction from the current situation.

Nina was so far away now, and even though he knew she had betrayed him—had betrayed all of them—he couldn't stop thinking of her.

Was she okay? What did she remember? Why had she lied to them?

The ship took another dip, and Tim began to think he might need that throw-up tube himself.

"Everything is fine," Rusty shouted back at the kids. He tried to calm them by explaining that the wild ride caused by Earth's atmosphere is actually a good thing for them because it's caused by particles of air rubbing against their ship, causing it to slow down so they can approach Earth at a safer speed.

"It's called friction," he continued. "It might not feel good right now, but you should certainly be thankful we're experiencing it."

The words had barely been said when suddenly a shrill alarm sounded overhead.

"We are going in a bit hot," Canary said to Rusty in a low voice.

Without another word, Rusty closed the door to the cockpit.

Tim looked over again at Max, Emily, and Luke.

"What did he mean . . . hot?" asked Emily.

"Probably referring to the fire outside the window," said Luke, who appeared somewhat calmer than the others. Probably, Tim thought, because he had been through it before.

"Was it like this when you came to Earth the first time?" Tim asked.

"Well sort of," Luke replied with some hesitation. "But . . ."

"But what?"

"Well, I don't remember seeing fire—and we didn't have an alarm go off."

Tim closed his eyes again and held on tight.

Chapter 2

Do They Look Like Us?

Are we dead?

When you actually have to ask the question and you really don't know the answer, you can bet you've been though something intense.

Impact was sudden.

The spacecraft appeared to nosedive toward the bright blue water of Earth before plunging deep under the glassy surface before coming to a full stop on the murky ocean floor.

"Are we dead?" Tim managed to ask again, certain that because no one answered the first time, he probably was.

Canary laughed.

"No, Tim," he said as he put a hand on the young man's shoulder. "You are decidedly not dead."

Canary and Rusty had opened the cockpit door moments after landing and were now helping everyone undo their safety belts.

"We're going to take the ship to the underwater docking station, but there's no need to be buckled in any longer," Rusty said. "Is everyone feeling okay?"

They all nodded in response.

Tim stretched his arms up in the air and walked up to a window. Looking out, he could see an ocean that looked very similar to his on Indus—except for what appeared to be something alive out there.

Wait. What the . . . ?

"Look out here," he called toward his friends.

They all huddled around the small window.

Emily jumped back when she saw it.

It was a squiggly, wiggly, squishy looking thing—almost invisible—and it was moving around right outside the window.

"That's called a jellyfish," Luke said. "There are a lot of living things in the oceans here on Earth: fish, sharks, dolphins, and whales—wait until you see one of those—you will definitely freak out."

"That's just weird," Emily said with a frown. "Yuck."

"Get used to it," Canary called to her. "It's just one of many new and different things about this planet—wait until you see the bugs."

"Yum, bugs," Max said. "I can't wait to eat some real food again."

Canary's stomach gurgled at the thought.

"Hey look, what's that?" Emily asked.

"What is what?" Rusty responded.

"It has eight—um—legs and a big head."

Rusty looked out and saw nothing like what she had described.

"It sounds like you might be talking about an octopus, Emily, but I don't see one."

"But it's right over there," she said pointing straight ahead.

Rusty grabbed a pair of binoculars and held them up to his eyes.

"Wow," he said with surprise. "There is an octopus out there—but I can barely make it out—even with the binoculars. How are you seeing that?"

"It looks really close to me," she answered.

Rusty made his way back to the cockpit and guided the vessel into what looked like an enormous underwater cave. Once fully inside, he brought the ship to a halt.

"Now, we wait," he said.

"Wait for what?" Max asked.

"Not for what, but for who," Rusty replied with a wink.

Suddenly the ship lurched upwards, as if a giant hand had just grabbed it from underneath and was lifting it up, up, up.

Tim could see they were indeed rising, like being on a supersized elevator.

After a few moments, they came to a stop, and the water around the ship began to lower.

"They're here," Canary said as he turned to Rusty.

"Wait . . . Rusty," Max whispered. "Do they . . . um . . . do they look different from us?"

"Well, Max, I do have to mention something very important," he replied. "Whatever you do, don't look at their third eye. It's actually a laser beam that can turn you to mush."

"What!" Max yelled out.

"He's kidding with you," Luke said with a laugh. "Man, you are so gullible."

Canary turned to Max and gave him a playful push on the shoulder.

"They look just like you—ugly as sin."

Rusty walked to the hatch and began to enter some sort of code.

They heard a loud banging coming from the outside.

"Come in," Canary jokingly called.

Tim felt a wave of panic rising in him. After all, he didn't know anything about these people. What if it had been a mistake to come here?

A few bells sounded, and the hatch began to rise slowly.

Luke stood in front, alongside his father and Canary.

Instinctively, Tim, Max, and Emily all reached for each other's hand.

As the door rose higher, Tim could see there were at least ten people outside it.

They were all dressed in white, clinical-looking medical jumpsuits that covered their heads. The whole suit actually covered their entire body.

"They're dressed that way for safety," Luke said in a hushed voice as he turned to look back to his friends.

"Whose safety?" Tim whispered back. "Theirs—or ours?"

Before Luke could answer, one of the men boarded the ship.

"Welcome, everyone," he said. "Welcome to Earth."

This is going to be a huge shock for them.

"What is?" Tim asked as he looked at the man.

"I'm sorry young man, what did you say?"

"You said, 'this is going to be a huge shock for them,' I just wondered what you meant."

The man just stared at Tim with a confused, sort of surprised, expression.

Another person came onboard—this one looked more like a woman.

She walked past the other man and stood in front of Tim, Max, and Emily.

Up close like this, they could all see her face clearly now. She took a moment to look at each of them warmly and then softly spoke.

"Welcome home."

Chapter 3

What a Weird Place

Earth.

What a weird place.

One sun in the sky, green trees everywhere, and the bugs were so small, they actually gave Tim the creeps.

And everywhere he went, he kept thinking people were speaking to him. But when he would turn to look at them, they were not talking.

He was beginning to think he could read their thoughts. But that was crazy, right?

This planet was definitely going to take some getting used to.

Since their arrival a few days ago, Tim, Emily, and Max had been given a crash course about Earth. There were many similarities to Indus. But all Tim could see at the moment were the differences.

The group had been staying on a huge compound that consisted of one large glass building and other various structures that housed some of the planet's military operations and offices.

The glass building was where he and his friends were staying. Every single wall was a window, but you couldn't see in from the outside—Tim had tried. The building almost blended right into the sky.

They each had their own comfortable room there with a huge bed and a private bathroom.

Everyone was being super nice to them, treating them like they were extremely special. Tim was beginning to believe they were.

Just one thing bothered him: the place seemed to have an awful lot of security. There were guards everywhere, all across the compound, throughout the building, and outside every door—including his.

And if he had to find one other thing wrong with the whole set up, he would have to say the food. They ate strange things here on Earth. The things they called "hot dogs" bothered him the most. They were just gross. And peanut butter and jelly was beyond disgusting—the bread here was so sweet, like cake. Soda was strange, too. He imagined it was exactly what the acid tasted like in his school science experiments.

Each day they had been here they had attended some sort of class where they learned about their new planet. Max called it Earth School.

They had learned a lot already.

Tim couldn't believe that the planet had around 195 different lands, called countries. And each country had its own individual territories. America alone had fifty separate places that they called states.

What a difference from Indus and its five regions.

Earth also had a lot less water than Indus.

Water covered about 70 percent of the surface here.

Today's session was about the customs here.

One thing that Tim had already noticed was that everyone says hello like they are familiar with you—even when they don't know you at all. They learned that this is a nationwide phenomenon in America. You could be greeted by dozens of strangers as you walk down an average city street here—all smiling and waving at you—and not know a single one of them.

The speaker, whose name was John, also explained to them that when someone you don't know says, "Hey, how you doing?" it's more of a greeting than a question wanting an answer.

Max had raised his hand on that one.

"So you mean as I'm answering this person's question, letting him know how I'm doing, he's already gone?"

"Yup," John had replied. "Long gone. It's basically as if he's saying 'hi.' He most likely does not really want to know how you are actually doing."

He also told them about holidays, which all seemed very odd to Tim.

Max couldn't get over the fact that in America, they stuff themselves with a crazy looking bird named Turkey.

Emily loved the whole story of Christmas but didn't understand how a pine tree with presents underneath was connected to it.

Tim was blown away at the one called Halloween where kids dress up as goblins and demand candy from strangers. It seemed like people on Earth trusted strangers a bit too freely.

With the session over, John looked exhausted. They had asked a lot of questions and still had more.

"I know there is a lot left to learn about Earth," he said kindly. "But you will learn most of what you need to know firsthand—by living your new lives here."

Tim liked John a lot.

He was patient and reassuring. Tim felt like he could really talk to him—trust him.

He quickly realized he had just admitted to himself that he now trusted a person who was basically a stranger.

Wow, he thought. I've barely been on Earth a week and I'm already acting just like them.

The facility had a huge yard in the center. Trees, grassy hills, and a lake right in the middle complete with fish and a few mean ducks.

Canary had stopped by Max's room earlier and asked him to meet him outside after lunch. As Max made his way outside, he could see Canary though the large floor-to-ceiling window that overlooked the park area. He was tossing a ball up in the air and catching it with a big glove.

"Hey," Max called over to him as he walked outside. "What's up?"

"Hey, yourself," he said as he quickly threw the ball over to Max.

Max tried to catch it, but it whizzed right past him instead.

Canary threw another ball and this time Max caught it—but then it popped right in his hand.

"Whoa little man—you're strong!"

"I can't believe I just broke your ball—I'm sorry."

"Sorry? Don't be sorry!" He laughed. "Haven't you ever had a catch before, man?"

"Uh, no. I guess not."

"So there's no baseball on Indus?"

"Baseball . . . no."

"Well, Max, today I'm going to teach you all about America's pastime."

Canary picked up the bat and motioned for Max to move farther away.

"Okay, I'm happy to learn. But I have to know —what is your real name? It can't be Canary."

Canary laughed.

"I don't share my real name with anyone. But I'm going to make an exception for you," he said. "It's Spike."

"What?" Max laughed. "You're kidding."

"Yeah, I am. Now go stand over there and get ready to hit this ball with that bat."

Max held the bat up and when Canary threw the ball, Max hit it—hard.

The ball flew out of the park and over the highest building.

"Max, you have quite the strength—you're like Superman or something."

"Super—who?"

"Ha, never mind Max, just get ready for the next one, okay?"

He did what he was told, and when the afternoon was over, he realized it was one of the best days he ever had.

≈ ≈ ≈ ≈ ≈

Emily was the last one left in the cafeteria.

Everyone eats so fast here, she thought to herself. She couldn't wait to see her sister Isabelle. She had missed her so much, and she was told that tomorrow they would get to see each other. Emily was so excited.

"I see you are the last customer," a woman said from behind.

"Oh, hi, Stacey," Emily said. "I'm sorry, I'll go now."

"No, Emily, please don't," Stacey pleaded. "I'd . . . I'd really like it if you stayed."

Emily looked at her for a moment. It was strange. Stacey seemed sad, but also happy—all at the same time.

"Stacey, are you alright?"

"Yes, honey, I just thought maybe we could talk awhile. You and your friends have been through so much."

Emily thought a moment and realized she did need to talk—and not to boys. She missed her mom on Indus terribly and being with Stacey made her feel a bit better.

They began to talk. The words came easy. And before either of them knew it, several hours had passed.

It was nice to have a new friend, Emily thought.

Chapter 4

Meet the Family

They would all have special visitors today.

Family was coming to see them—real family.

Emily and Tim joined Max in his room to talk about it.

Max nervously paced back and forth.

"I'm not sure how I feel about this," Max said. "I mean I'm not sure I want to meet them."

Tim had to admit that he agreed.

"I know what you mean, man—we don't know these people at all."

Emily jumped up off the bed where she was sitting and walked to the huge pane of glass overlooking the lush gardens below.

"I'm excited," she said with a huge smile. "I get to see Isabelle today."

Tim and Max walked over to her.

"We're really happy for you," Max said. "Group hug?"

Emily laughed out loud and grabbed them both around the neck for a squeeze. They hugged her back.

"Ouch, Max," Emily teased. "You have a really strong grip."

Then there was a knock at the door.

Max walked slowly over and opened it.

John was standing there.

"Okay, guys—it's time."

"Two guys and a girl," Emily chided.

"Oh, of course, Emily," John laughed. "It's a saying here on Earth—saying 'okay, guys' can refer to both girls and boys."

Emily chuckled.

"Okay then, let's go, girls," she said gesturing at them.

"Um, well, it doesn't really work that way," John said. "Like I said, there's a lot more to learn.

They all laughed.

The three friends followed John down the long hallway to the elevator. They got on and took it to the highest level where there was a large meeting room.

When the doors opened, they entered into a beautiful sitting area with a waterfall in the center.

"This is our stop," John said as he exited.

Tim, Max, and Emily didn't budge.

John turned to face them.

"I know this is hard, but I promise it won't be as hard as you think."

Something about that statement made them all feel better, and one by one, they stepped off the elevator.

John led them over to a comfortable set of couches and motioned for them to sit down.

"Okay, here's how this is going to go," he began. "Someone will come and take each of you to a separate room where you will meet your parents."

"My sister, Isabelle, is here, right?" Emily anxiously asked.

John smiled.

"Yes."

Max put a gentle hand on Emily's back, and then turned to John.

"How long will we be with them?"

"It's completely up to you," John responded. "No one is being forced to do anything they are not comfortable with. You will remain here at this facility, and if you want to go stay with them for a visit, that is encouraged. The goal is to eventually let you go back home—to live."

"Home?" Max said wistfully. "Home feels pretty far away right now."

"Baby steps," John said before realizing that was probably another confusing metaphor.

Just then, a young woman entered the room.

"Emily?"

Emily jumped up.

"Well, here I go! Wish me luck."

"Good luck, Emily—give Isabelle a hug for us," Max called after her as she followed the woman down a long hall.

When they got to the end, the woman opened a door and held her arm out, gesturing for Emily to go inside.

When she did, she could see that Stacey was there sitting on a couch. Isabelle was right next to her—close—and holding her hand.

"Isabelle!" Emily called to her sister. "I'm so happy to see you!"

She ran over and embraced her tightly.

"Oh, Emily, I missed you so much."

They hugged and laughed and talked for about an hour.

Emily had forgotten Stacey was even in the room until she said something.

"I'm so happy you are together again," Stacey said reaching for Isabelle's hand.

"Oh, Stacey, I want to thank you for being here, too," Emily said. "But where are my . . . my Earth parents?"

"Emily!" Isabelle said with a laugh. "This is our mom. Stacey is our mom!"

≈≈≈≈≈

"Max?"

This time it was a young man.

"Max, follow me please."

Without responding, Max dutifully got up and followed him down the same hall.

"Third door on the right, buddy," the man said.

Max walked to the room and went inside.

"My real name is Reginald," Canary said. "But if you ever call me that, I'll whoop your butt."

Max laughed.

"What are you doing here, man?"

"I'm your brother, Max."

≈≈≈≈≈

As Tim stared out the window, he felt a light tickle on his arm. A tiny black bug with little wings had landed there. He jumped up from his chair so quickly that it toppled over on its side as he swatted the grotesque creature off.

"It's okay, Tim," John said. "It's just a pesky fly—quite harmless."

"Yuck," Tim said with disgust. "Well, I guess my parents forgot me."

"No, Tim, they didn't," John said.

I'm your father. I really hope you are not disappointed.

"Wait, you're my dad?" Tim said standing up.

"How did you know that? I didn't even say anything!" John said with amazement.

"I heard you, you said you were my father and you hoped I wasn't disappointed."

"Tim, you didn't hear me—you read my mind. I thought that—I didn't say it."

"I have been hearing a lot of things lately," Tim said.

"Well?" said John.

"Well what?"

"Are you disappointed?"

"No, I'm ... I'm actually really happy it's you."

Then Tim reached out, and they hugged each other for a very long time.

Chapter 5

New Beginnings

Together the three friends sat in silence. They were lost in their own thoughts.

Rain fell softly against the window outside the comfortable room where they had gathered after each meeting a member of their "real" families. Other than the gentle hum of the building's ventilation system, the room was hushed.

Max finally broke the quiet as he got up from the overstuffed chair where he had been sitting and walked to the window.

"Well, I never would have guessed in a million years that the stranger we ran from—

the one we thought was out to kidnap us—would turn out to be my brother."

"I can't say I saw that one coming either," Tim said with a laugh. "But you have to admit, he's pretty cool."

"So is your dad," Max said as he turned to walk back to the chair. "That sounds *so* weird—*your dad.*"

"Isabelle looked so happy. I was so relieved to see her safe, and Stacey seems really nice—but I can't bring myself to call her *my mom*," Emily said without taking her eyes off the floor. "I really miss my mom and dad on Briny Deep."

"It's okay, Emily," Tim said holding out his hand which Emily quickly took. "I feel the same way. It's just so—*weird.*"

Max leaned forward and put his hand atop both of his friends.

"Yeah, it's definitely going to take a long time to get used to this," he said with a smile. "But we'll always have each other, and we'll make it through together."

Just then, the door opened and Luke came in to join them.

"Hey, are you all doing okay?"

"*Okay* might be a stretch," Max answered with a wink. "I'd say we are pretty far from okay, but we'll get there."

"I understand," Luke said as he took a seat next to Emily. "Even though my dad hasn't changed, he's not really the same person I thought he was. I mean, he's like some sort of secret agent."

"How is everything going with your brother —and your mom?" Emily asked.

"It's really good. I mean, at first I couldn't believe it—even after I saw them for the first time, but now it's just—*normal*."

Luke got up and walked back to the door.

"You'll all get to your normal place, too. It won't always feel so strange . . . but . . ."

"But . . . what?" Tim said as he stood and walked over to Luke.

"It just might get a little stranger before it gets normal. Today you are going to visit your homes—meet some other family members," Luke's voice trailed off as he opened the door and took a peek outside.

"However, first—I have some old friends I thought you might want to see."

Luke opened the door wide, and in walked Anthony and Eva. Isabelle tailed behind laughing and skipping along.

They all hugged each other for what seemed like forever—and then began sharing stories about everything that had happened.

Turns out Eva and Anthony had been here the whole time, just staying in another building across the courtyard.

After a while, John came into the room and called Tim over.

"Good to see your friends again?" he asked.

"Yes, really good," Tim replied.

"I want to invite you all downstairs—we have something we need to talk to you about," John said as he motioned to the door.

They all followed him out and down the hall to another room Tim hadn't seen before. It was another large meeting room—but it was filled with people in uniforms.

Probably military, Tim thought.

They all took a seat and then John started to speak.

"We have observed something extremely remarkable in each of you," he began. "You each seem to possess a special power here on Earth."

The kids all looked at each other puzzled.

"I thought it was just me who was hearing things," Tim said.

"No, Tim, each of you has a separate gift—Max is showing unbelievable strength, Emily can see very far distances, and her sister, Isabelle, is able to hear things from very far away."

"You mean every one of us has something?" Eva asked.

"Yes, Eva. We have not determined what you, Luke, and Anthony can do—but we will be testing you tomorrow, and we'll find out."

"How cool!" Anthony shouted.

"Okay, everyone, that's it for now—just wanted to make you aware that we will be conducting more tests on all of you. We are not sure whether these extraordinary powers are only effective here on Earth—or perhaps they are now a permanent part of your chemistry."

Isabelle raised her hand.

"Yes, Isabelle?"

"Will the tests hurt?" she asked.

"No, of course not, sweetheart."

"Oh, thank goodness!" she called out.

Laughter filled the room.

As everyone started to leave, John faced Tim and put his hands on his shoulders.

"Are you ready to meet your mother?"

"My mother?" he asked. "Yes . . . I think so."

The drive to his old house took less than an hour. As they drove down the wooded road, Tim could see it just ahead.

It was yellow—the same house from his dreams.

"I remember," he said softly. "I ran here, trying to get home. But someone was chasing me. I was too slow."

"No, Tim, you were just a little boy. You tried—but you didn't have a chance to outrun a grown man."

John pulled the car up a small hill, past rows of flowers and into the small driveway.

A woman was standing in the doorway. She quickly burst out the door as the car came to a full stop.

"Oh, Matthew!" she cried out.

Tim slowly opened the car door and got out.

He didn't recognize her at all, yet as he moved a little closer, there was something familiar about her.

She ran to him and embraced him tightly. He hugged her back as tears began to fill his eyes.

"Mom?"

"Yes, it's me, Matthew—oh how I've missed you."

"Mary, he's called Tim now," John said softly as he wrapped his arms around them both.

"Tim?—I don't care what your name is now," she said letting go for just a moment and looking him in the eyes. "You are my son, and I won't ever lose you again."

They spent several hours inside talking—his mother showed him all the things he use to have as a boy. It appeared she had not thrown one thing of his away despite how many years had passed.

Tim was most surprised by his old room. The room of a toddler, his room had remained the same all this time later. A drawing he must have made in school still hung proudly on the wall. Toy airplanes, which must have been a favorite of his when he was younger, were everywhere, and his clothes still hung in the closet.

She never gave up hope, he thought.

When the time came to head back to the facility, Tim's mother gave him another long hug.

"Soon, you will be coming home for good, understand?"

"Yes . . . Mom, I'll be home again soon."

As Tim and John drove away, they took another little road out. John slowed the car as they began to approach a school.

"Tim, that was your school," he said pointing to the small tidy building.

"Can I please go look?" Tim asked.

"Yes, of course."

He pulled the car into the parking area, and Tim quickly got out and walked over to the building. He passed the front entrance and went to the fenced area out back. It was a playground.

He knew this place.

"I had a teacher here I loved, I remember her!"

"And I remember you, Matthew."

Tim spun around to see an older woman standing there, wait . . . it was Mrs. Wol . . . ? What was her name—he knew it.

"Ms. Wolpert!" he called out.

"Yes, it's me. Oh, Matthew—oh, I'm sorry. Your dad just told me you go by Tim now. Oh, Tim, I'm so sorry this happened to you . . . I should have been watching you."

"No," he said. "Please don't be sorry—you were my favorite teacher."

Then they hugged—a good, long hug.

After taking a tour of his old school and talking a bit longer, they said their good-byes.

On the drive back, Tim was puzzled.

"Why do I remember her, but not you or Mary . . . I mean Mom?"

"They must have wiped your memories of us completely away, or at least tried very hard to," he said with a frown. "They didn't realize you had developed a strong bond with someone else—Ms. Wolpert. That must be why you dreamed so often of the schoolhouse and running from it—deep down you remembered something, or someone, here."

As they reached the grounds of the facility, Tim hugged John good night and made his way up to his room.

He immediately got into his pajamas and slipped under the covers of his bed—exhausted.

He didn't know much of what the future held at this point, but he was *sure* of one thing—he would never dream of the yellow house again. He didn't have to. He had found it.

Chapter 6

Surprise Visit

Ms. Duvall sat by the window and peered out onto the street. People walked by very fast these days, and she rarely saw a child outside.

Things in Briny Deep were changing very fast.

With all these missing kids, no one was above suspicion anymore—except perhaps *her*. After all, how could an old woman who couldn't walk be of any harm to anyone?

That last thought actually made her laugh out loud.

Truth be told, she did have to be very careful. Her colleague, Mr. Kull, was under a certain degree of scrutiny, although like her, his age made him less of a target as well.

Her work here had been very useful to the agents back on Earth. By using the tunnels, she was able to slip unnoticed back and forth throughout town. She had focused her surveillance on several people who had recently begun to meet secretly—or so they thought—twice each week at an old abandoned warehouse on the outskirts of town. They disguised themselves with hooded coats so she had yet to identify any of them—except Nina's parents. It was them who had led her to the group in the first place. She had been watching Nina's home since the kids had made their escape, and it had finally paid off one night.

Leaving her disguise as an old woman behind and using specialized listening devices, she had determined the group was either responsible for, or aware of, kidnapping the children from Earth. But someone else who wasn't present at these clandestine meetings—someone with much more authority—seemed to be the one really calling the shots.

She had heard his name—or at least a nickname. He was called Trident, which was strange considering the trident was a three-pronged spear used on Earth many years ago for fishing, and also the weapon of choice for many of Earth's mythical Greek gods including the Greek god of the ocean, Poseidon.

She had her suspicions of who he really was. She thought he might be the regional commander of Briny Deep. If that was true, his real name was Edward Gorgon, and he was very powerful.

At the last meeting, she overheard something very troubling.

They were talking about the kids who had been brought back to Earth. Someone said they had powers now—extreme strength, advanced eyesight, and superhuman hearing. One of them even had the ability to read minds.

How did they find this out? She had wondered. Then she realized.

They must have a spy on Earth.

And that spy must have access to the kids. This was information she must get to Rusty immediately.

So far, it had proved impossible to follow any of the other people at these gatherings to their homes after the meetings so she could identify them. But tonight would be different.

There was a meeting tonight, and she would be there in the shadows—listening.

Just then a loud banging came from the cellar. Duvall quickly closed the curtains and made her way toward the cellar door. Her feet creaked on the old wooden floor. When she reached the door, she held her hand out towards the knob and then froze in place—she could hear footsteps coming up the stairs. She withdrew her hand, took a step back and reached for a weapon—she kept several various weapons within close proximity at all times. An old habit she wasn't about to change anytime soon. The closest to her at the moment happened to be a bat. But not just any bat—her favorite saying was written in big black letters across the length of it—*Don't Mess With Texas.*

This will do just fine, she thought.

The doorknob was turning. She readied the bat.

As the door opened, a man loudly shouted out, "I don't plan to mess with Texas!"

"Kull!" she called to him. "I'm going to knock your clock clean off one of these days! Why didn't you notify me that you were coming?"

"My apologies, but I had to see you immediately, and the phones are not a safe place to speak freely," he replied. "We got word that the kids arrived safely."

"Well, that's great, but that can't be why you snuck in without warning," she said feeling a tiny trace of anxiety.

"No," he said seriously. "We have trouble, big trouble."

"Okay, but you have to tell me quickly—the targets are gathering again tonight, and I have to leave soon to get there in time.

"You can't go," he said slowly.

"What? Why?"

"Because they know—*they know who you are.*"

She stared at him with surprise.

"What do you mean, they know?"

He threw up his hands in frustration as he lowered himself onto a red love seat.

"I was combing through Nina's house and came across a letter. It had your name under a list of suspects," Kull said.

"But why would they suspect me?" she said loudly. "To them, I'm just an old woman."

"I don't know, but they have you down as a suspect," he answered. "I already told Rusty and he's coming back."

"There's more I have to tell you," Duvall said. "The kids on earth have developed special abilities, and the people I've been watching know about it."

"But the kids just got back—any abilities that were discovered must have just been documented," Kull said. "That means that someone there on Earth is communicating with someone on Briny Deep."

"Yes," Duvall responded. "They are getting immediate updates from someone."

"We have to tell Rusty," he said. "Now, let's go."

A loud banging on the front door interrupted his sentence.

"Go, now!" Duvall said motioning downstairs.

"Come with me!" he said as he rushed to the basement door.

"I can't. They will search the house and find the entrance to the tunnel. Listen to me—the files I've been keeping are in the safe downstairs —you know where it is. It has all the children's records of being born on Earth and tapes of all the conversations I've recorded of that group."

The banging on the door became louder.

"You must leave now!"

He nodded and disappeared into the cellar.

Quickly she rushed to her wheelchair and adjusted her wig—but it was too late.

The door was broken down within seconds, and the men came rushing in.

"There's no need for the disguise," a large burly officer said. "We know who you are."

Chapter 7

Going Back

Bright sunlight poured in through the window of Tim's room. The rain had finally stopped. It looked like it was going to be a beautiful day here on Earth.

Tim jumped out of bed and showered. Today, Rusty was meeting him and the rest of the kids from Briny Deep for another meeting. And he said it was a very important meeting, so no one should be late.

Every meeting they had seemed to be an important meeting.

As he walked out his door and down the hall, he noticed how neat and clean everything was. He didn't mind it here. He actually really liked it a lot. The huge building was like a little town or a city. He had his friends here with him. There were places to eat and a lot of nice rooms to meet with the others to hang out and relax.

Tim had no idea when they would all go live at their own homes.

Now that they knew about their special abilities, they were all being studied by the scientists here. Over the last week, they each had to take silly tests and answer a lot of questions every day. But he didn't really mind. Everyone was very nice about it, and they were even trying to help him control his ability.

Being able to hear someone else's thoughts was not something he considered a gift. Most of the time, it filled his head with jumbled words when he walked by a group of people, and he couldn't really make out who was thinking what.

But the scientists were starting to show him how to control it. Soon, they said, he would be able to turn it on and off. Tim definitely wanted to turn it off.

They also said that he would be able to make the things he heard clearer so that they made more sense. Tim trusted them. But he kind of wished he had Max's power—strength. Now that was cool! He also wondered what powers Eva, Anthony, and Luke had. He would have to ask them today.

Tim took the elevator down to the bottom floor. There was a big room there where they had lots of meetings. He walked in and saw Rusty and Luke sitting at a table in the back. Luke looked upset. They were talking so low, Tim could not hear what they were saying.

"Tim," Rusty called over. "Come in, join us."

Emily and Isabelle were arm-in-arm, laughing and smiling. It was nice to see them so happy. Max and Luke each grabbed a seat close to the door. Rusty walked over to Luke and put a hand on his shoulder, then walked to the podium at the very front of the room. Eva and

Anthony walked in last—they seemed to have become really good friends now.

"Thank you everyone for joining me," Rusty began. "I know many of you are missing your parents from Briny Deep."

"I am," Emily said.

"Me, too," Eva added.

"Yeah, I think we all miss our parents," Anthony chimed in.

"Well, I want you to know that they will all be here soon," Rusty said. "We have a plan to bring them all back to Earth because they miss you, too."

Relief and joy filled the room as everyone clapped in approval.

"Wow, two sets of parents," Tim whispered to Max who smiled back at him.

"I have some other news to share," Rusty said.

Tim felt a pit in his stomach. Why was he so nervous all of a sudden?

"I am returning to Briny Deep tomorrow," Rusty continued.

"Wait . . . won't the police arrest you?" Max asked.

"No, as far as anyone knows, I've just been traveling between regions," he answered. "I travel all the time, so no one should think it's strange that I've been gone."

"But why do you have to go?" Isabelle called out. "Why must you go back?"

"We have another child to rescue and our agents who are there now may be in trouble," he said. "I need to help them."

Tim stood up from his seat.

"You can't go alone."

"I have to, Tim. I can't draw any suspicion to myself by showing up with a new face."

"Let me go with you."

"No. We can't risk losing you there," Rusty said firmly. "I just wanted you all to know the plan. I promise I'll be back soon."

～～～～～

The very next day, the kids all gathered to see Rusty off. As he boarded the ship, Luke ran over to give him one last hug.

"I can help you," he pleaded. "Let me come."

"No, Luke," Rusty said. "We took a risk bringing you back once; I won't take that risk again. Things are getting bad in Briny Deep."

They stopped hugging, and Rusty looked his son right in the eyes.

"Take care of your mom. I will be back."

"Okay, Dad, just please be careful."

"Always."

As Rusty's ship left the underwater docking station, the kids watched it push through the dark ocean waters. Once it was out of sight, they all ran upstairs to the observatory where they had a clear view of the sky. They made it just in time to see the ship fly off into the clouds on its way to Indus.

"Well, there he goes," Emily said. "Do you think he'll bring our parents back with him?"

"I don't know," said Luke. "This seems like an emergency trip, so I'm not sure. What do you think, Tim?"

Luke turned and looked around the room.

"Hey, where's Tim?"

Chapter 8

Trident's War

The man with jet-black hair stared out the window of his large office. It overlooked Briny Deep's town center. It was so beautiful here, and he would do what he had to do to protect it. And if that meant upsetting a few people, so be it.

There were five very important people sitting behind him who were waiting for his instructions. He kept his back to them. Because even though they were important, he was the *most* important man in town.

As regional commander of Briny Deep, Edward Gorgon had control over everything here. At least that's what he liked to think. He did not take kindly to anyone getting in the way of his plans—and he had big plans.

"Sir," one of them finally said. "We need to make a move quickly."

The man slowly turned to look directly at the one who had spoken.

"You don't think I know that?" he snapped. "But we have to make the right move."

"We know when he's arriving, we have him on our radar," said a serious looking woman. "We can take him into custody the moment he lands."

The man turned his gaze to her.

"Then do it, and bring him right to me."

"Yes, sir."

"And one more thing—I do not want to be called Commander Gorgon anymore. You will now call me Trident. Now go!" he barked at everyone in the room.

They quickly filed out.

Yes, he liked that name much better. The Trident was a weapon used by the ancient

mythical gods of Earth. And that's what he was
—the great and awesome weapon of Indus—
the one that would save them all.

~~~~~

As the ship roared toward Indus, Rusty pushed
the auto pilot button and removed his safety
harness. He stretched his arms above his head
and yawned. Then he stood and walked to the
back of the vessel.

"You can come out now," he called. "I know
you're onboard."

Tim emerged from the shadows.

"How did you know I was here?"

"Because I can see the weight of the ship and
there was extra weight—enough to add up to a
young man."

"I had to come, I had to try and get Nina to
come back to Earth with us."

"But do you realize how much your family
on Earth is going to worry? They just got you
back."

"I know, I thought about that—but this is
just something I have to do."

"Well, we can't take you back to Earth now, so I guess we need to try and change your appearance a bit," Rusty said, sounding a bit annoyed. "We're dyeing your hair blond—bleaching it."

"And you have the stuff to do that onboard?" Tim asked.

"I'm always thinking ahead," Rusty replied. "Now, let's go do this."

It only took a short time to dye his hair. And when it was finished, Tim looked in the mirror. He actually thought it looked pretty cool.

"Hey, I look like Canary," he laughed.

Rusty went back to the front to maneuver the ship through one last wormhole. After about an hour, he returned to the main cabin.

"Well, Tim, we're here."

Tim hurried over to the window and looked out. There it was—his other home. He had only just left, but it felt like a long time ago. So much had happened.

The ship made a gentle landing into the soft waters of Indus. Tim thought it was much nicer than his descent to Earth. As the ship glided through the water, Rusty called him over to give a few last minute warnings.

"Remember to wear the coat I gave you and keep the hood up around your face as much as you can," he said. "And stay close to me at all times. Don't do anything without telling me first. Understand?"

"Yes, and I am sorry I put you in such a tough spot, but I promise I won't get in the way."

"You've been through a lot more than any boy your age should have to, Tim," Rusty said with a sad smile. "I just hope this wasn't a mistake for you."

Then, he returned to the captain's chair and guided the ship into the same dock they had used before.

"No one is here now. We'll hurry through the city and catch a late shuttle to Briny Deep. It should be empty this time of night," Rusty said. "Go to the storage in the back and grab my bag. I'll meet you outside."

Tim rushed to the back. He looked for the door to the storage room.

He found it and ducked inside, grabbing the only bag he could find. As he made his way back to the front, he heard shouting. It was coming from outside the ship.

He peered out the window and saw at least ten men surrounding Rusty.

They were police.

Rusty was trapped!

Chapter 9

Run for Your Life

Tim stayed very still. He thought about his options, but he realized that there was nothing he could do to help Rusty. There were just too many men. If he went out there, they would simply capture him, too. He knew he had to hide, but he was sure that the police would search the ship for other people. Where could he go? Was there a back door off this thing?

Outside, the men had already put handcuffs on Rusty. Peering out a window, he could see several of them approaching the ship. Rusty looked scared. Tim ducked down slowly. He looked around for the best place to hide. He didn't see any back doors, but there were a lot of bins throughout the cabin used for storage. However, they were way too small for him to fit in.

He ran to the back area where the storage room was. He quickly slipped inside the door and looked around for a place to hide. He decided on a large box with several coats inside. Tim lifted out the heavy coats, climbed in the box, and then pulled the coats back on top of him.

He could barely breathe under the weight of it all.

Loud noise filled the ship—voices and the sound of heavy feet coming down the aisle. The men were onboard. They would most certainly find him!

Tim was beginning to really regret his decision to come along.

Then, he heard the door to the storage area squeak open. The men were inside the room. He heard boxes being moved and kicked aside.

Tim could also hear his heart pounding in his chest, and he was sure the men would hear it, too.

"No one else is here," one of the men shouted out.

It sounded like they were leaving.

Had they left the room? Tim wondered. Nope, it still sounded like someone was there.

I think someone is in this box.

Wait, Tim thought to himself. Did I just hear someone's thoughts? Here on Briny Deep?

The coats were lying right on his face. His nose began to itch.

Oh no, he thought.

And then it happened—he sneezed—loudly.

He heard footsteps approach the box where he was hiding. Then, someone lifted the coats off of him. Tim realized he was going to get caught. And there was no escape.

Suddenly, Tim was staring right into the eyes of a police officer.

The man staring back at him looked surprised.

"Listen to me carefully," he whispered. "I'm Steve, I'm Rusty's friend. I couldn't warn him about this arrest because I didn't know it was coming until it was too late."

Tim wasn't sure he was hearing him right.

"You aren't going to arrest me?" he asked, his voice cracking.

"No, of course not, but if those guys out there find you, they definitely will take you into custody. You have to stay here. I will come back later when it's clear and get you out."

"Can you help Rusty?"

"No, he's being held in a cell at the Reef Institute. I don't think I can reach him there. I can't really even help you much more than getting you out of here. I have a family I need to protect. Now duck back down and I'll cover you up again. Remember—stay put until I get back."

And then he was gone.

The noise outside began to fade away. He was alone, in a box, on a ship.

The seconds became minutes. The minutes became hours and soon he felt his legs begin to go numb. He had to get out of this box. But what if someone was out there?

Tim slowly pushed the coats off his face and to the side. Then he listened.

Silence.

Tim slowly lifted himself out of the box and felt his legs begin to tingle from being asleep. They were stiff, so he shook them briskly and they began to come back to life. Raising his arms over his head, he stretched out and began to feel like he could move normally again.

The grave circumstances he now found himself in began to sink in.

What was he going to do?

Steve had never come back. Should he try and make it out on his own?

Tim knew he had to try. He couldn't wait any longer. It would be morning soon and others would be arriving in this building for work.

He knew it was a huge risk, but he had no choice.

With his newly blond hair and a hooded sweatshirt, he just might have a chance to make it back to Briny Deep—and Nina.

But would she want him back?

Tim opened the door to the storage room and peeked outside. Then he slowly walked down the aisle of the ship's cabin to the front. When he got to the front, he peeked out a window. There was no one out there. The room was dark again. It must still be night.

And there was still no sign of Steve. He really wished he had his phone.

Time to go, he thought.

Pulling the sweatshirt up over his blond hair, he walked off the ship and headed for the elevator. Tim was just about to press the button for it, when he realized it might be better to take the stairs.

He saw the stairwell just ahead and started heading up.

After several minutes, he could tell this was the longest staircase he had ever climbed. *Maybe I should have taken the elevator.*

It was too late now, so he kept climbing, and climbing, and climbing. Up, and up, and up.

Man, will this thing ever end?

Finally, it did. And Tim found himself in the front reception area of the building. He quickly made his way outside and searched for signs of the shuttle.

Rusty had handed him a shuttle pass while they were still onboard the ship, so he wasn't worried about getting on the shuttle. He was more worried someone would see him and wonder what some teenager was doing out by himself in the middle of the night.

He was also concerned about finding the shuttle station. Having traveled this route with Rusty before, he tried to remember the best way to go.

Finally, he made it to the station and it was almost empty. One old man sat on a bench and another older couple walked hand in hand on the other side of the room. Thankfully, he was able to slip onto a shuttle without being seen.

Tim sunk down into a chair in the back.

He was on his way back to Briny Deep.

Chapter 10

Nina's Choice

Nina paced nervously back and forth.

She wanted to listen to her parents' conversation downstairs but was afraid what else she might learn. Moments ago, she had accidently heard them talk about the night Tim, Max, and Emily had disappeared. They had said she was there when it happened?

But, how could that be?

The last thing she remembered was talking to Tim at school. He was in a hurry to get somewhere—but she couldn't remember where exactly.

And then he was gone.

She should have followed him. Wait . . . that sounded familiar. Did she follow him? The whole day was a huge blur to her. It almost felt like it had been wiped away from her memory.

Maybe she could have saved them if she had told them the truth. But she had agreed to keep the secret from her friends—that they were from Earth. Her parents had explained to her what a terrible place Earth was and how much Indus needed them to keep growing its population. It made sense to her. And she didn't want them to ever leave. But lying to her friends had not been easy. Acting like she didn't know the truth was hard, especially when she started to develop feelings for Tim—strong feelings. And when all the kids started disappearing, she knew what was happening—Earth was coming back to get them.

But now, why were her parents whispering?

They had always told the truth about everything—*didn't they?*

She tiptoed over to the stairs and walked halfway down.

"We have to do something fast," her mother was saying. "There are spies everywhere. The whole thing is going to unravel."

"Trident has a plan. We need to stick with that plan," her father answered. "It will cover the whole thing up, so the other regions won't know the truth."

"We shouldn't have to get caught up in this. We are scientists," her mom responded.

Her father walked over to her mother and took her hand.

"Lisa, we are responsible for this experiment. We convinced Trident to orchestrate the kidnapping of all of those children from Earth so we could see if they would thrive here," he said softly. "We didn't tell anyone in the capital city of Nomad—we didn't inform any of the other regions. If we are caught, we could get in a lot of trouble. Now, we have to cover it up."

"But a war?" her mother whispered back.

"If we had been able to finish our work, we could have saved our planet from eventual extinction," her dad answered. "But it was interrupted too soon. Now we have to act like it never happened."

"Okay," she replied. "But Nina must never know that she's from Earth, too."

Nina stumbled back a step when she heard that last line.

Tears welled in her eyes. She was from Earth, too?

She didn't understand anything they were saying, but she knew she had to get out of there.

Nina crept down the rest of the stairs, slipped over to the kitchen, and snuck out the back door. Then she ran, and ran, and ran.

She had no clue where she was going. She just wanted to get away. All those years, she had never felt particularly close to her parents. They were always working. Over the years, she had tried to impress them with good grades and her loyalty. But they always seemed distant and unemotional.

Now she knew why—they were not her real parents!

She was some sort of experiment gone wrong.

Nina found herself running in the woods. She had no idea where she was. Then she saw it—Rusty's cabin. She must have been running a long time, so she plopped down on a nearby log, cradled her head in her hands, and sobbed.

"Nina?"

A familiar voice called from behind.

"Nina, is that you?"

She slowly lifted her head and turned to see who was saying her name.

"Tim!" she cried as she ran over to him and hugged him.

Tim's arms remained at his side. Nina had betrayed him—had betrayed them all. As much as he wanted to hug her back, he couldn't.

"Where have you been? I've been so worried about you! Are the others with you?"

Then Tim remembered that Mr. Kull had wiped her memory of that day at the cabin when he learned she had been lying to them all along.

He removed her arms from around his neck.

"Nina, I know you lied to us. You knew we were from Earth. You knew we had been kidnapped. But you never said a word."

She took a step back and her eyes filled with fresh tears.

"I never wanted to lie to you. My parents told me . . . well turns out they're not my parents . . . they lied to me. Tim, I'm from Earth, too."

He stood staring at her for a moment—in shock. How many more secrets were there?

Tim couldn't stand to see her in so much pain. She was a victim, too, only doing what her parents—her kidnappers—had told her to do all these years.

He stepped forward and swept Nina into his arms, holding her tight.

"Nina, we have a lot to talk about, but right now, we need to get to the tunnel and find Mr. Kull. I think he's the only one who can help us now."

Chapter 11

The Story Gets Twisted

Rusty was handcuffed to a chair.

All he could do was sit and watch the man with black hair pace back and forth in front of him. He knew the man well but not by the name he was now using—Trident.

Rusty knew him as the highest official in Briny Deep—the man in charge of everything here. He was the top man, also called the town's regional commander.

Each region had a commander. They made the laws, enforced the rules, led the police, and ruled over the other officials in town. Rusty had respected him, trusted him. But he had tricked

Rusty. He was a bad man—the one responsible for all of the kidnappings on Earth.

In charge of all the regional commanders was the chief who lived in Nomad.

Rusty was tired of waiting for Trident to speak.

"Does the chief know about your little experiment?" he asked briskly.

"Of course not," Trident said with a laugh. "He doesn't know what this planet needs. He is weak. And once I take over, things will change. Indus will be strong."

"Once you . . . take over?" Rusty stammered. "You really are crazy."

"My experiment is the only thing that could save this planet. In ten years, there will be no more children born on Briny Deep unless we bring in children from other planets to grow up here, marry here, and have their own children here. By joining with compatible species, the population on Indus will continue to grow. I am the only one who can save this planet!"

"Save it by kidnapping children from their real parents? That's not saving anyone—that's a crime and you have to be stopped."

Trident laughed again.

"And who is going to stop me—you? By this time tomorrow, I will have a declaration of war approved by the chief against Earth."

"Against Earth—for what?" Rusty said in disbelief as he struggled with his cuffs.

Trident moved closer to Rusty until he was just inches away from his face.

"For kidnapping *our children,* of course. For aggressively attacking our planet with thugs who took our beloved children away in ships."

"That's a lie!" Rusty yelled. "You would start a war just to cover up your own terrible plan?"

"I would start a war to save my planet," he replied. "And I plan to save it by taking over power from the chief once we declare war. He will look weak for allowing all these children to be taken over the years. The people of Indus will need a new leader—me."

Then he called for two men to take Rusty to a cell.

"I'll find a way to stop you," Rusty shouted.

"You're not going to stop anything," Trident called after him as he was led away. "You are a spy who has been helping Earth in its devious plan—you are going to jail for a long time."

"You won't get away with this," Rusty yelled out. "There are too many good people on Indus —they would never let you be the chief."

"Ah, but you underestimate how many people are already on my side," he hissed. "And once I harness these special powers I'm hearing about on Earth, there will be no stopping me."

"How did you hear about that?" Rusty said as sweat dripped from his brow. "That's not true."

"Oh, but it is true," Trident bellowed. "My spies tell me the kids are exhibiting special powers on Earth—guess that means I would have them, too!"

Then Trident turned to the men from security.

"Take him away," he ordered.

≈≈≈≈≈

As Nina and Tim ran through the tunnel, Tim tried to remember which hatch led to Mr. Kull. Along the way, he told Nina all about Rusty being captured and his escape from Nomad.

"It was scary, but no one noticed me and as soon as I got to Briny Deep, I headed for the tunnels," he said breathing heavily. "I was heading for Rusty's cabin when I found you. I thought about going to my parents, but I didn't want to get them in trouble."

Tim stopped by a hatch.

"Wait, this one leads to Ms. Duvall," he whispered. "She can help us, too."

They climbed up the ladder to the hatch, opened it, and climbed inside. They were in her cellar. It was dark and musty.

A noise from the corner startled them.

"What are you two doing here?" Mr. Kull demanded.

"I came back with Rusty."

"Rusty is here?"

"Yes, but . . . he's been captured."

For the first time since he met Mr. Kull, the man looked scared.

"So has Ms. Duvall. I came back to see if they found her safe with some of our papers inside, but luckily they didn't."

"Rusty said he was here to rescue someone else," Tim said.

"Yeah—it was Nina."

Tim and Nina looked at each other in surprise.

"It was Ms. Duvall who found out Nina was one of the kidnapped kids," he explained.

"She's been watching her parents for a while now—broke into the house and listened to a few of their conversations."

"They lied to me all this time," Nina said.

"Yes," Mr. Kull said. "There are a lot of people in this town who have lied. And we have to get you two back to Earth fast. Things are getting bad in Briny Deep, really bad."

Using the tunnels, the three of them made their way to the hatch leading to Nomad. Once on the shuttle, Kull used his phone to call someone, and after a few minutes of conversation, he turned to them.

"I've arranged another ship on the other side of the city for you since the one Rusty used to get here is being watched," Kull said. "I'm going to have someone I trust meet you there to pilot the ship back."

When the shuttle came to a stop, they followed Kull through the city, taking back alleys and keeping out of sight as much as possible.

Finally, they arrived at a small building. They went inside and took an elevator down to the lowest level. When they exited, Tim saw the ship. It was much smaller than the one he had been on before.

"This is it. This is your ride," Kull said. "No time for good-byes."

"But what about Rusty and Ms. Duvall?" Tim asked.

"Don't worry. I'm not leaving them behind," Kull answered. "Now go."

Tim nodded and then held out his hand.

"Thank you, Mr. Kull. You're not so mean after all."

Kull shook Tim's hand firmly.

"No," he replied. "I am, and the people who took Rusty and Ms. Duvall are going to see just how mean soon enough."

Chapter 12

War and Peace

Trident leaned over the shoulder of the chief as he read the charges.

"We need to have your signature on this right away, sir," he coaxed. "A ship was just reported leaving our airspace—a ship with more of *our children* on board."

The chief bellowed back at him.

"Why was I not made aware of this situation earlier?"

"Sir, we just found out that Earth was responsible for the abduction of all the children who went missing in Briny Deep," he calmly responded. "They are taking them to use them in some sort of dangerous experiment—we must send warships now before it's too late."

"It certainly is an act of war to take our children," the chief agreed. "And according to these charges, you have proof that they intended to take hundreds more?"

"Yes, sir, they are trying to destroy Indus by taking the only future we have left."

As the chief signed the paperwork, Trident placed a call.

"Send the warships to Earth now."

≈ ≈ ≈ ≈ ≈

They placed Ms. Duvall in a cell just across from Rusty.

"I see they got you, too," he called to her.

"I just hope they didn't find the safe," she whispered back. "All the proof we have is in there."

"Let's hope Mr. Kull gets to it first," Rusty replied. "Quiet—someone's coming."

The sound of footsteps echoed down the long hall of cells—all of them empty except for two. They were getting closer, but it was still too dark to see who it was.

For a moment, Rusty thought he saw Trident. If he was coming, they were in trouble. It meant he didn't need them anymore because he had found and destroyed all the evidence Ms. Duvall had hidden away. He would now want to get rid of them for good.

As the shadowy figure approached, Rusty could see it was a man.

"Steve," Rusty said with a sigh of relief. "I can't believe you made it inside."

"When I went back for the kid, he was gone," Steve said apologetically. "I was scared to help you at first, but I realized I had to—this craziness can't go on anymore."

Steve quickly unlocked the two cell doors.

"Come with me, and stay close," he said quietly. "We're meeting up with Mr. Kull. He has the papers."

"I'm so relieved," Ms. Duvall said.

"Listen carefully, its bad—the regional commander of Briny Deep is behind everything —he's convinced the chief to declare war on Earth—*for taking Briny Deep's kids.*"

"We need to get the proof of their birthplace on Earth to him right away," she responded.

"I have a car waiting outside to take us to the shuttle station," Steve offered.

"Tell the driver to take us to this address," Rusty said as he scribbled an address on a tiny scrap of paper. "This is the closest hatch to the tunnel. From there we can get past security and catch the shuttle fast."

"Tunnel?" Steve asked looking puzzled. "Well, as long as it will get us past security, let's go. They will discover you're gone soon and come after us."

~~~~~

As their ship docked safely on Earth, Tim quickly escorted Nina off the deck.

John was there to meet them. He ran up to Tim and hugged him.

"I won't get into how reckless it was of you to stow away like that right now," he said sternly. "But only because we have bigger things to worry about."

"I know, they have Rusty—they have a whole plan to destroy Earth!" Tim shouted.

"You'll need to come with me and tell us everything you know," John said. "But when I say bigger things to worry about, I mean *that*."

John pointed out the huge window and up to the sky.

Four large warships hovered just overhead.

Tim and Nina were whisked into a conference room where they shared all the information they had with a roomful of people from military intelligence.

"I just received information that Rusty and Duvall have escaped," a short man with a thick mustache said. "They are attempting to get to the highest government official with proof of a cover up."

"Let's hope they get there very soon, otherwise we are going to have to protect ourselves with all available force," a tall man with white hair said. Then, turning to another man who was holding a bright red phone, he added, "Scramble our fighter jets, now."

≈ ≈ ≈ ≈ ≈

Trident was victorious. He couldn't help but smile widely as he watched the radar and saw his warships had reached Earth.

His warships—that sounded so good. It wouldn't be long before everything was his. He had a lot of support—people that were afraid to speak out publicly—but who would gladly come out of the shadows once he gained control of Indus.

The chief would be laughed out of office once everyone knew he did nothing to protect their children from being taken, and that it was Trident who had finally taken action.

And if he didn't agree to step down—well then—Trident would push him down and take over by force. Either way, he would win.

Once he had control of Earth, they would simply take over and all the children would be his. They would become the new children of Indus, and they would be forced to bow down to him.

≈ ≈ ≈ ≈ ≈

After being escorted from the meeting, Tim looked at John and could see he was nervous.

"It's too late," John whispered. "They are sending jets up now. Once they start shooting at each other, it won't matter who started it in the first place—we will be at war."

"What do we do?" Tim asked.

"I want you and Nina to head down to the shelter on the bottom level with the other kids," he answered softly. "They are going to attack this building first—maybe there you might have a chance."

"But what about you?" Tim pleaded. "You have to come, too."

"I have to stay up here, Tim," he said. "This is what I do. If anything happens to me, I want you to know I feel so blessed that I got to know you, even if it was just for a short time."

"Wait, look!" Tim shouted pointing up to the sky.

The warships from Indus were pulling away; they pulled up into the sky and disappeared into the clouds.

"What does it mean?" Tim asked.

"I can't believe it," John said. "It looks like they are retreating."

≈≈≈≈≈

The door to the office where Trident was sitting burst open and several security officers surrounded him.

"What is going on here?" he asked with outrage.

The chief walked in the room, followed closely by Rusty, Steve, Ms. Duvall, and Mr. Kull who was holding a large stack of papers.

"What's going on is that you are going to jail," the chief loudly replied. "We have proof of your crimes right here." He pointed to the stack of papers Kull was holding.

Trident jumped up and pushed past security, knocking Kull to the floor, and ran from the room.

"After him!" called the chief.

≈≈≈≈≈

They all gathered in a huge reception hall.

"Okay, everyone listen up for a moment," a man in full military dress called out. "This has been quite a day, so I'm going to give you a chance to relax and just be with each other to celebrate this victory."

Everyone let out a cheer.

"But tomorrow we have work to do," he added. "With the discovery of so many special powers among you, we need to test everyone for theirs and see how we might be able to use them for the good of the planet. Agreed?"

Everyone did.

Surrounded by his friends—Max, Luke, Emily, Isabelle, Eva, and Anthony—Tim felt safe for the first time in a very long time. He knew his parents from Briny Deep would be arriving in the next few days, and he couldn't wait to see them! All his friends had parents coming in on the next ship—except for Nina. Her parents could not be located.

He watched as they laughed and hugged each other. It felt so good to be together again —all together.

Tim looked over at Nina. They had been through so much. He turned and walked to look out at a window.

I love you, Nina, he thought to himself, too afraid to say it aloud.

Suddenly, he felt a hand on his shoulder.

"Looks like we share the same special power," she laughed. "I love you, too."

≈ ≈ ≈ ≈ ≈

Somewhere in the desert of Arizona, a man with dark hair passed through a small town. It was evening. The sky was pitch-black, not a star in sight. Darkness covered the old, cracked concrete of the sidewalk where he walked, making it hard to see.

But he could see.

Turning to the bank on his right, and ignoring the "We're closed" sign dangling out front, Trident reached for the metal lock on the door—and it crushed to powder in his hands.

"Two special powers and counting," he said aloud. "Wait until I harness them all."

CPSIA information can be obtained at www.ICGtesting.com
Printed in the USA
LVOW06s1436120315

430302LV00003B/647/P